ED EMBERLEY'S

Drawing Book of

FACES

LITTLE, BROWN & COMPANY

LB kids

Little, Brown and Company

Hachette Book Group

237 Park Avenue, New York, NY 10017

Visit our website at www.lb-kids.com

LB Kids is an imprint of Little, Brown and Company. The LB Kids

name and logo are trademarks of Hachette Book Group, Inc.

First Revised Paperback Edition: August 2006

First published in hardcover in April 1975 by Little, Brown and Company

Library of Congress Cataloging-in-Publication Data

Emberley, Ed.

  Ed Emberley's Drawing Book of Faces / Ed Emberley

        p. cm.

  Summary: Simple step-by-step instructions for drawing a wide

variety of faces reflecting various emotions and professions.

  1. Face in art. 2. Drawing—Technique. [1. Drawing—Technique.]

I. Title. II. Title: Drawing Book of Faces.

NC770.E42   734'.49   74-32033

ISBN 978-0-316-78970-7

10 9 8 7

WKT

Printed in China

IF YOU CAN DRAW THESE THINGS→ •∪DOΔ□ℓℓℓℓ
YOU CAN DRAW ALL KINDS OF FACES.
EASY STEP-BY-STEP DRAWINGS SHOW YOU HOW.
THIS ROW SHOWS WHAT TO DRAW.
THIS ROW SHOWS WHERE TO PUT IT.

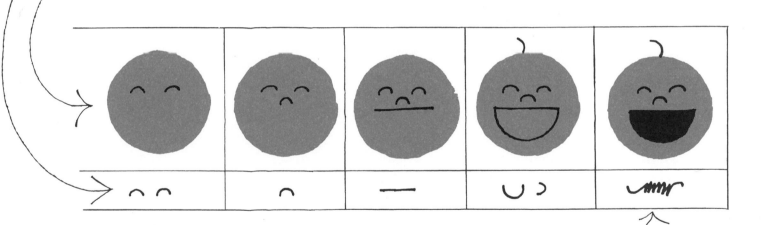

THIS SIGN MEANS "FILL IN"

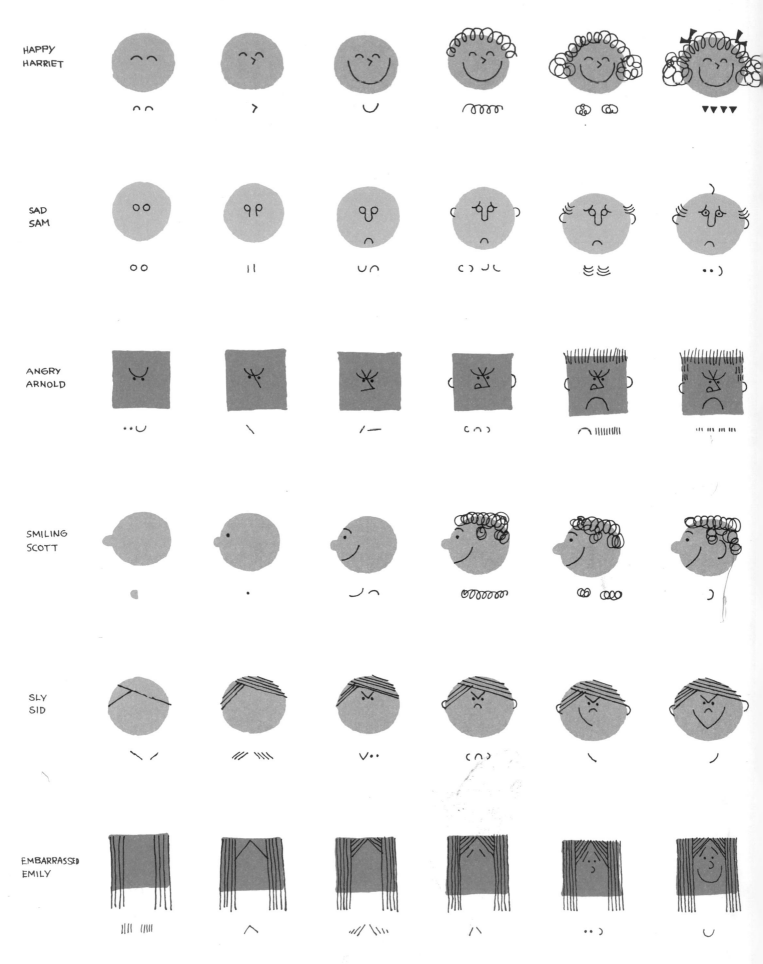

HAPPY
HARRIET

SAD
SAM

ANGRY
ARNOLD

SMILING
SCOTT

SLY
SID

EMBARRASSED
EMILY

4

GIGGLE GERTIE

SNOOTY SAMANTHA

PUZZLED POLLY

PROUD PAUL

TIRED TILLIE

 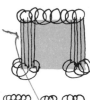   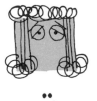 

LOVESICK LOU

 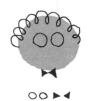   

LAUGHING
LENA

HOLLERING
HAROLD

DETERMINED
DAN

CONCEITED
CONROY

YUM YUM
YOLAND

GRUMPY
GWENDOLYN

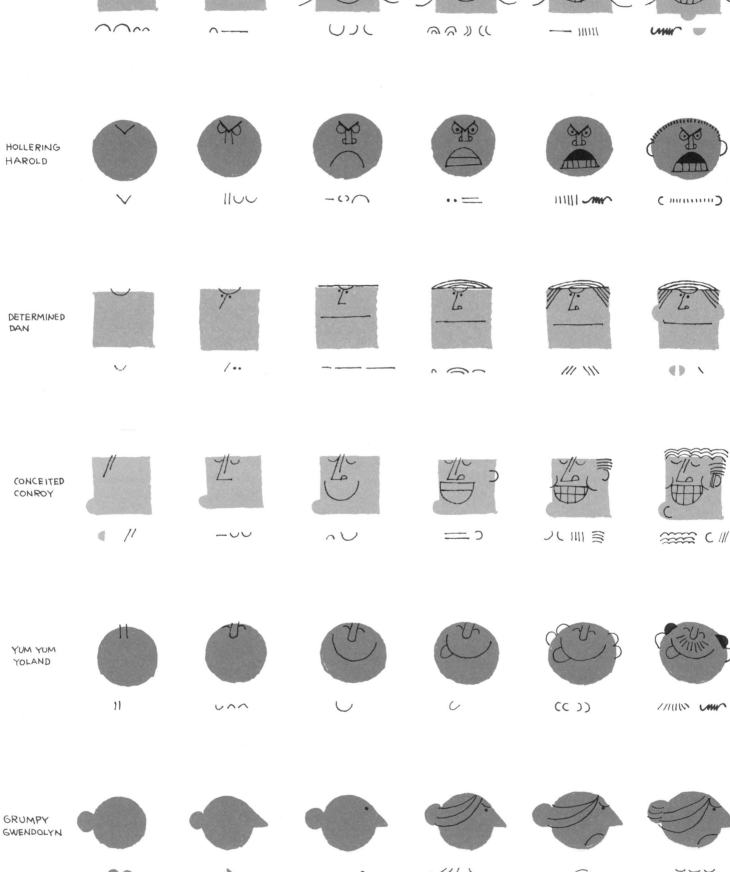

SLEEPING SIMONE

SNORING SALVATORE

SURPRISED SYBIL

FRIGHTENED FENWICK

    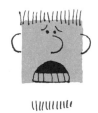 

MONSTER MELVIN

VAMPIRE VICTOR

WINKING WILLIE

WHISTLING WANDA

 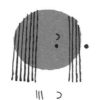 

YODELING YOLANDA

BARITONE BARNEY

COUNT CLARENCE

DOCTOR DIANE

8

TOUGH TOM

BABY BONNIE

PROFESSOR PIETRO

 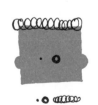  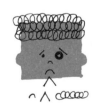  

FRECKLES FREDA

   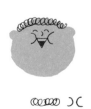  

BLACK EYE BOB

HEAVY HARLOW

WHISKERS WALDO

FUZZY FRAN

BRAIDS BARBIE

MEASLES MICHAEL

K.O.'D KARL

CURLERS CAMILLA

10

BEANIE BERNARD

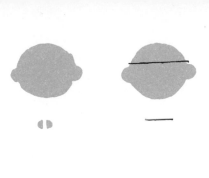   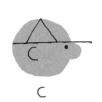  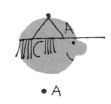

BASEBALL BILL

FOOTBALL FRED

EARMUFF EARL

STOCKING CAP SUE

GRADUATE GREGORY

11

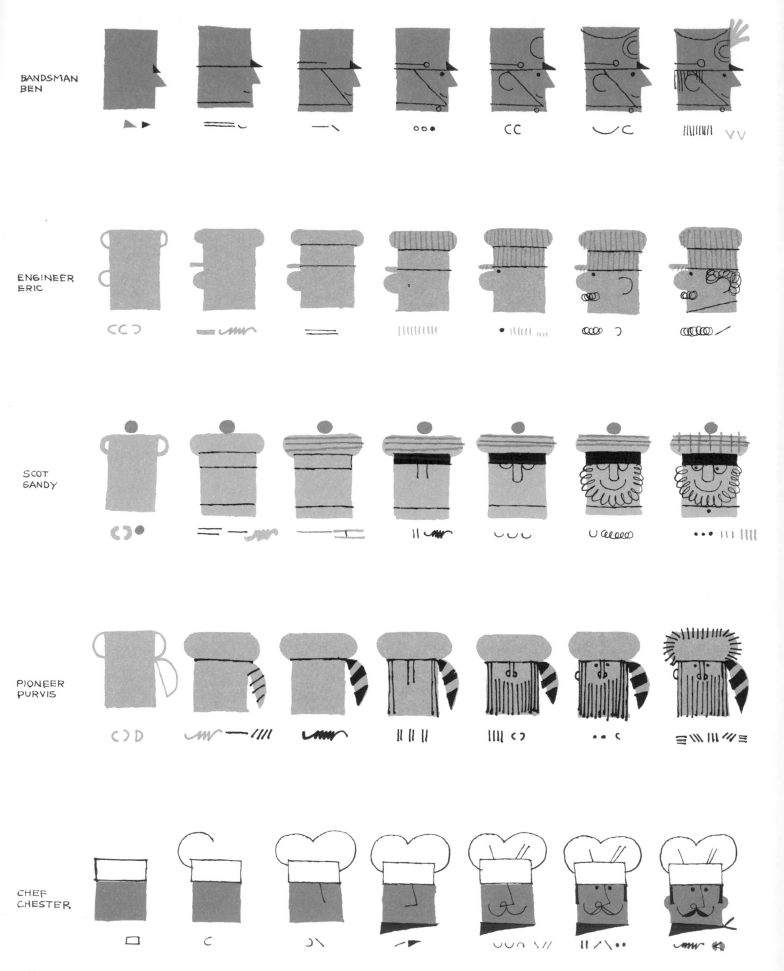

BANDSMAN
BEN

ENGINEER
ERIC

SCOT
SANDY

PIONEER
PURVIS

CHEF
CHESTER

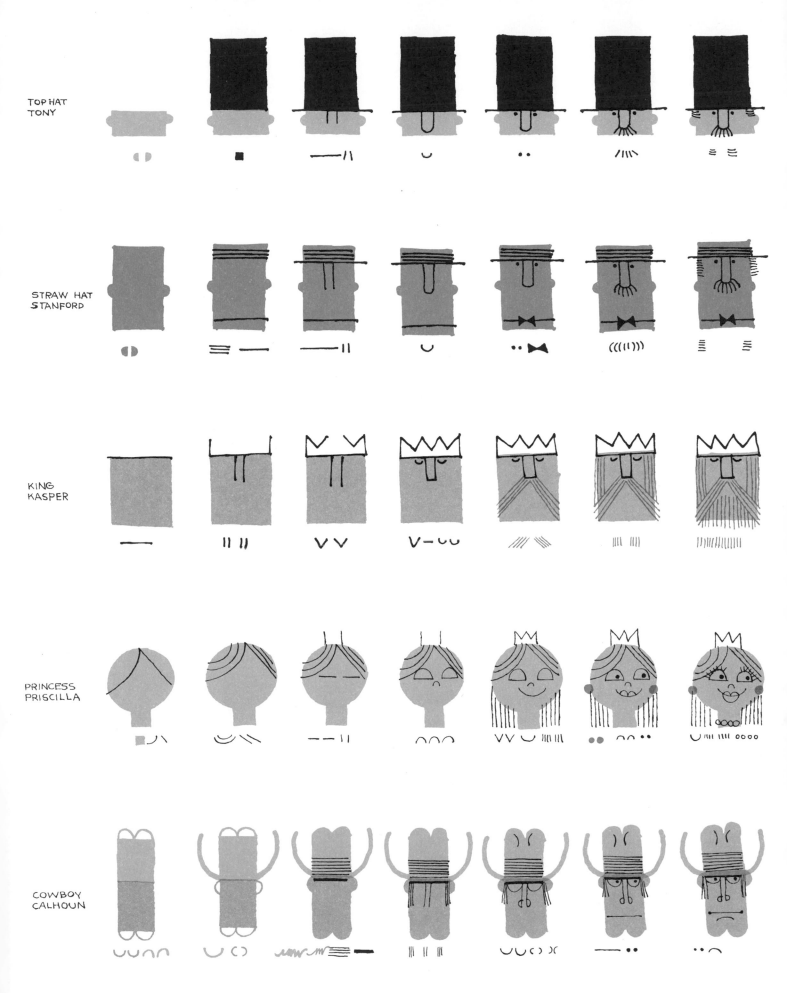

TOP HAT
TONY

STRAW HAT
STANFORD

KING
KASPER

PRINCESS
PRISCILLA

COWBOY
CALHOUN

13

TURBAN TALLIS

OFFICER OLIVER

   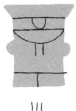   

METER MAID MAUD

ROBBER RUFUS

NURSE NORMA

14

STARLET
STELLA

ADMIRAL
ANDREW

SAILOR
STANLEY

SAILOR
STEPHEN

TOWN
CRIER
TOBIAS

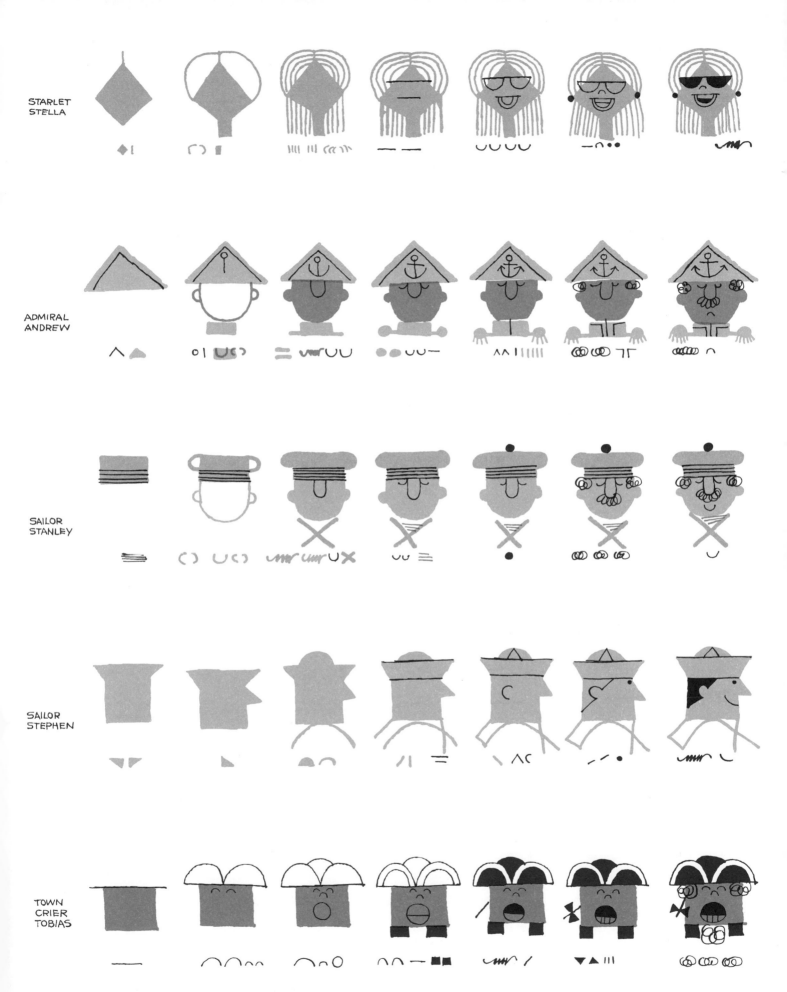

CLOWN CLAYBORN

CLOWN CORABELL

RINGMASTER RICARDO

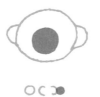     

MARTIAN MARTIN

DIVER DICK

WITCH
WILBERTA

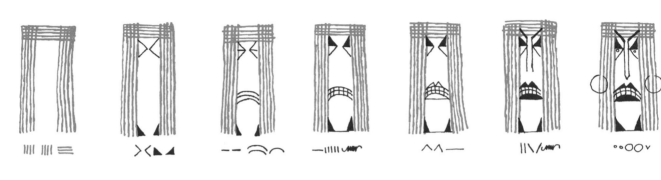

SPOOKY
SIGISMONDA

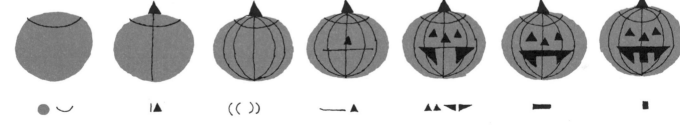

SKULL
SYLVESTER

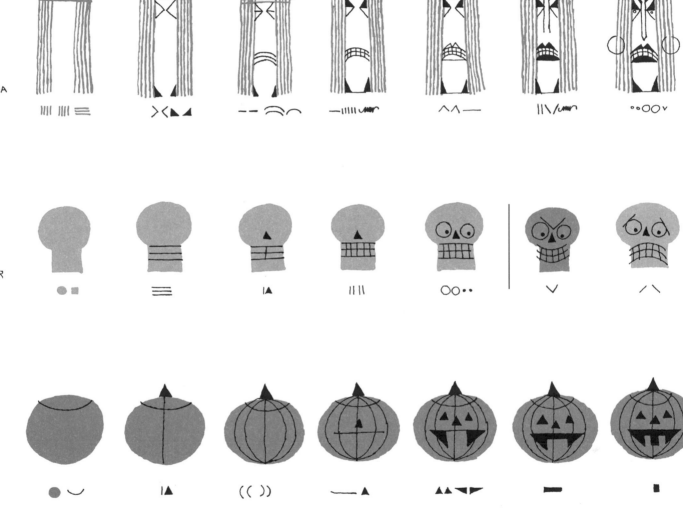

PUMPKIN
PANDORA

DEVIL
DUNWALTON

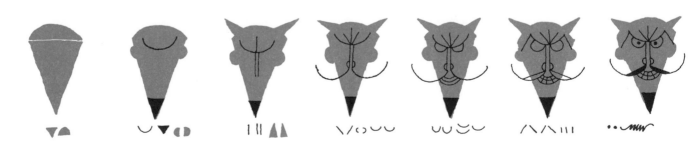

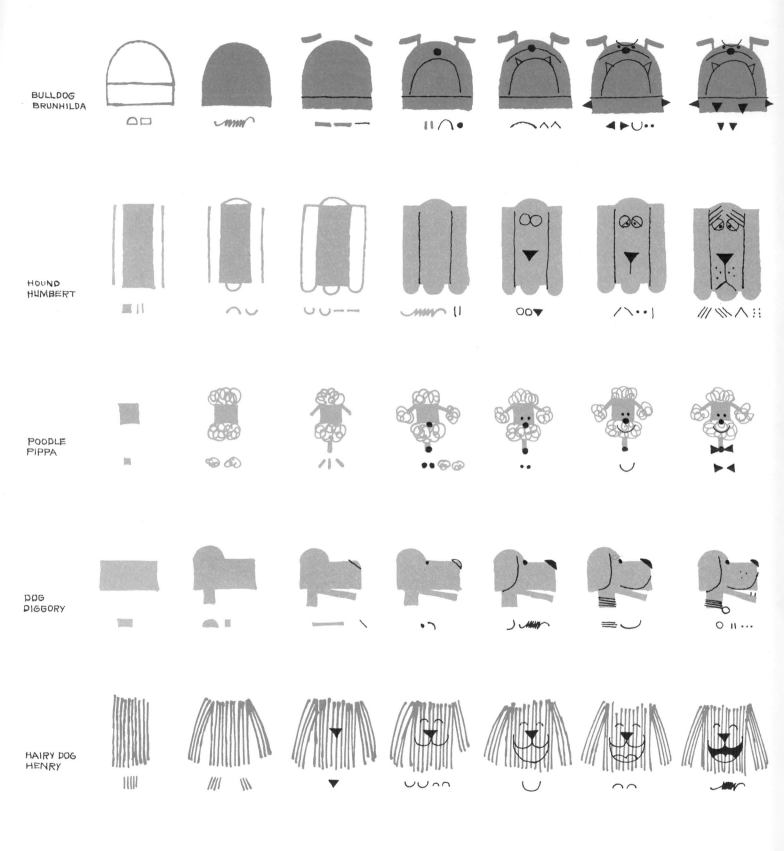

BULLDOG BRUNHILDA

HOUND HUMBERT

POODLE PIPPA

DOG DIGGORY

HAIRY DOG HENRY

ALLIGATOR ALGERNON

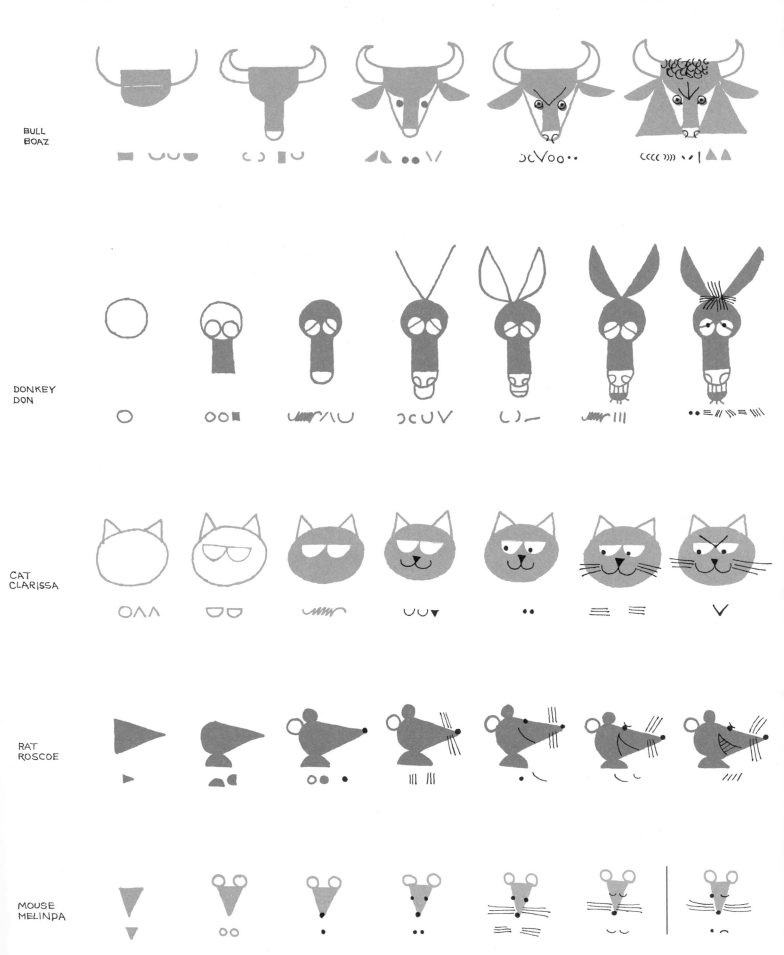

BULL
BOAZ

DONKEY
DON

CAT
CLARISSA

RAT
ROSCOE

MOUSE
MELINDA

19

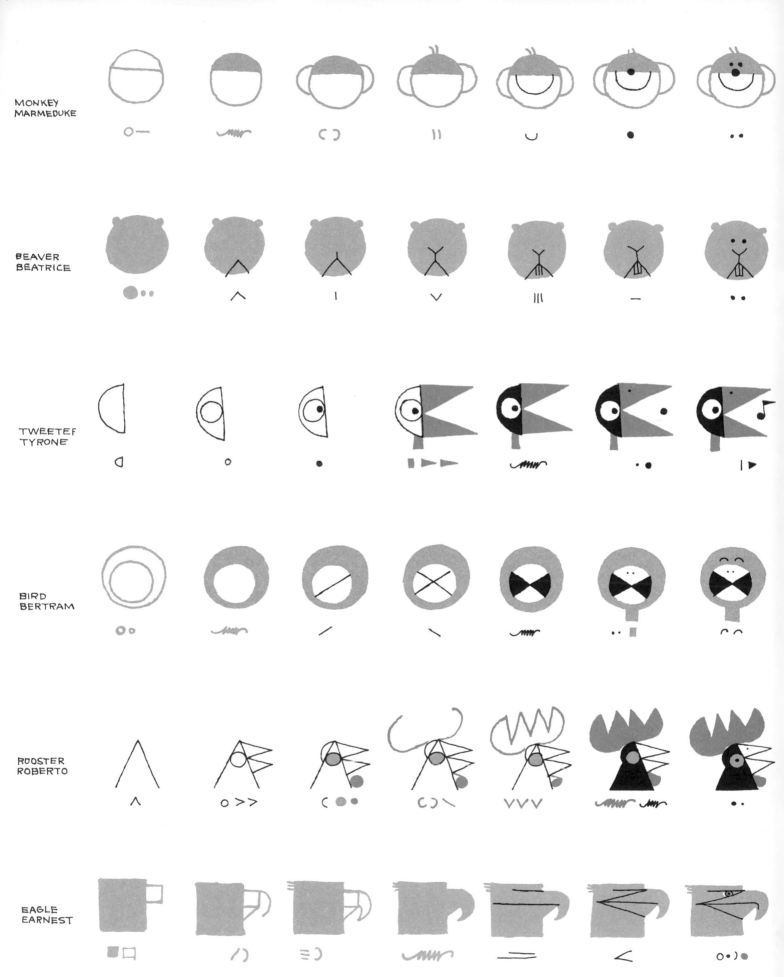

MONKEY
MARMEDUKE

BEAVER
BEATRICE

TWEETEF
TYRONE

BIRD
BERTRAM

ROOSTER
ROBERTO

EAGLE
EARNEST

20

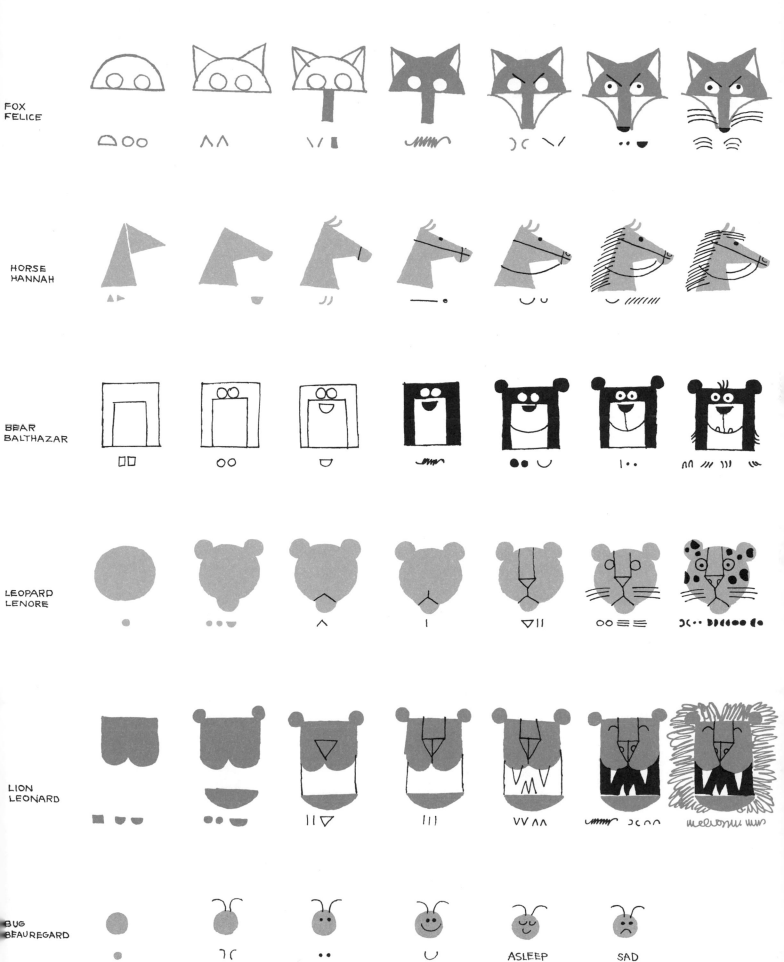

FOX
FELICE

HORSE
HANNAH

BEAR
BALTHAZAR

LEOPARD
LENORE

LION
LEONARD

BUG
BEAUREGARD

ASLEEP   SAD

21

★ HERE ARE SOME MORE FACES.
  CAN YOU FIGURE OUT HOW I MADE THEM?
  REMEMBER, THEY ARE MADE OF ○△□CD·I℮℮℮℮

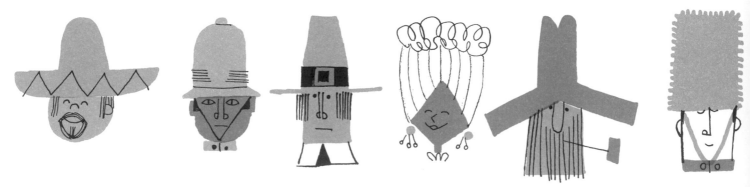

23

● ONE PART OF LEARNING TO DRAW IS TO LOOK AT REAL THINGS, PHOTOGRAPHS OF THINGS AND OTHER ARTISTS' WAYS OF DRAWING THINGS AND TRY TO DRAW WHAT YOU SEE. ANOTHER PART IS TO TAKE PIECES OF TWO OR MORE THINGS YOU LEARN TO DRAW AND PUT THEM TOGETHER TO MAKE A NEW THING. HERE ARE SOME WAYS FOR YOU TO MAKE "NEW THINGS" WITH THIS BOOK.

★ YOU CAN MAKE THE SHAPE TALLER...   ...WIDER...OR...

CHANGE IT...FROM SQUARE TO ROUND...

...FROM ROUND TO SQUARE....OR...

...... DIAMOND,   OR TRIANGULAR,   OR ANY OTHER   SHAPE YOU CAN   THINK OF.

★ YOU CAN CHANGE THE NOSE FROM ONE FACE TO ANOTHER.   ★ YOU CAN CHANGE THE HAIR FROM ONE FACE TO ANOTHER.

★ MOVING, SWAPPING, ADDING AND SUBTRACTING PARTS ARE ALL WAYS OF MAKING "NEW THINGS".

★ MORE NOTES AND HINTS:

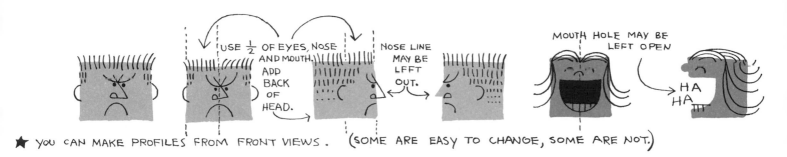

★ YOU CAN MAKE PROFILES FROM FRONT VIEWS. (SOME ARE EASY TO CHANGE, SOME ARE NOT.)

★ YOU CAN MOVE THE FEATURES UP TO MAKE THE FACE LOOK TOUGH OR DUMB, OR DOWN TO DO THE OPPOSITE.

★ TO MAKE A FACE LOOK YOUNGER MAKE THE NOSE AND EYEBROWS SMALLER, ALSO MOVE THE FEATURES DOWN.

★ TO MAKE A FACE LOOK FAT- KEEP THE FEATURES SMALL, CLOSE TOGETHER AND HIGH ON THE FACE.

25

NOSES

EYES

MOUTHS

26

HAPPY   WORRIED   ANGRY   EMBARRASSED   SHOUTING   SLY   LAUGHING   HUNGRY   DOUBTFUL

RPRISED   FRIGHTENED   HAUGHTY   SICK   CRYING   ASLEEP   OUCH   HAPPY   NOT HAPPY

EARS

HAIR

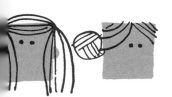   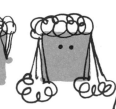 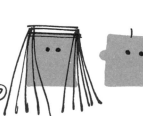

27

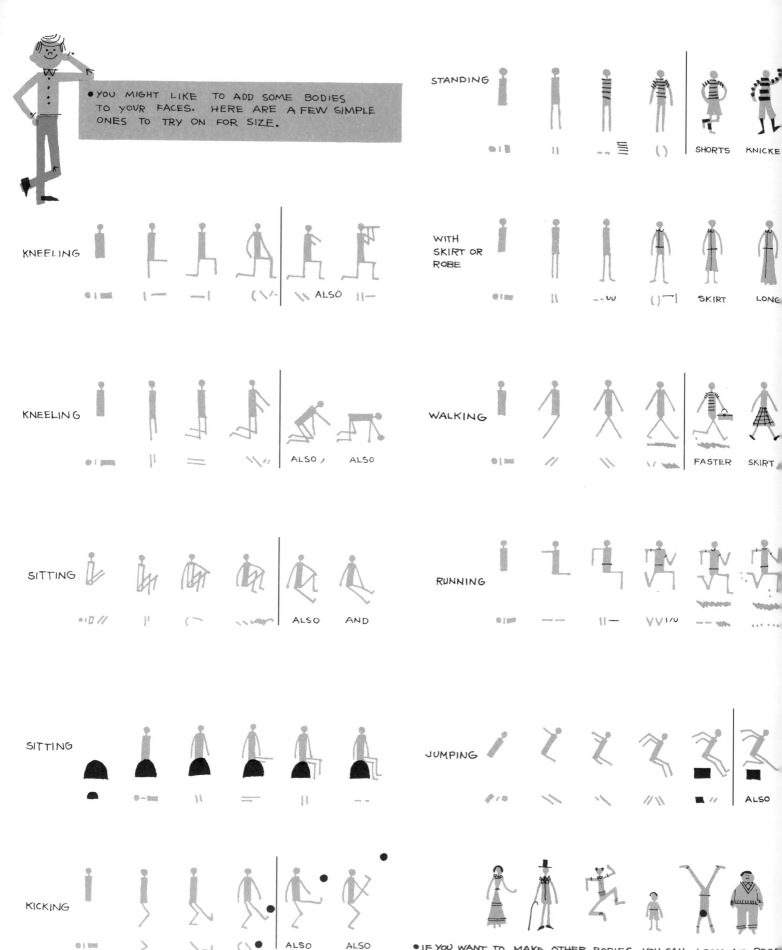

● YOU MIGHT LIKE TO ADD SOME BODIES TO YOUR FACES. HERE ARE A FEW SIMPLE ONES TO TRY ON FOR SIZE.

STANDING

SHORTS   KNICKE

KNEELING

ALSO

WITH SKIRT OR ROBE

SKIRT   LONG

KNEELING

ALSO ,   ALSO

WALKING

FASTER   SKIRT

SITTING

ALSO   AND

RUNNING

SITTING

JUMPING

ALSO

KICKING

ALSO   ALSO

● IF YOU WANT TO MAKE OTHER BODIES, YOU CAN LOOK AT PEO DOING THINGS, LOOK AT PICTURES, LOOK AT YOURSELF IN A MIRROR AND DRAW WHAT YOU SEE.

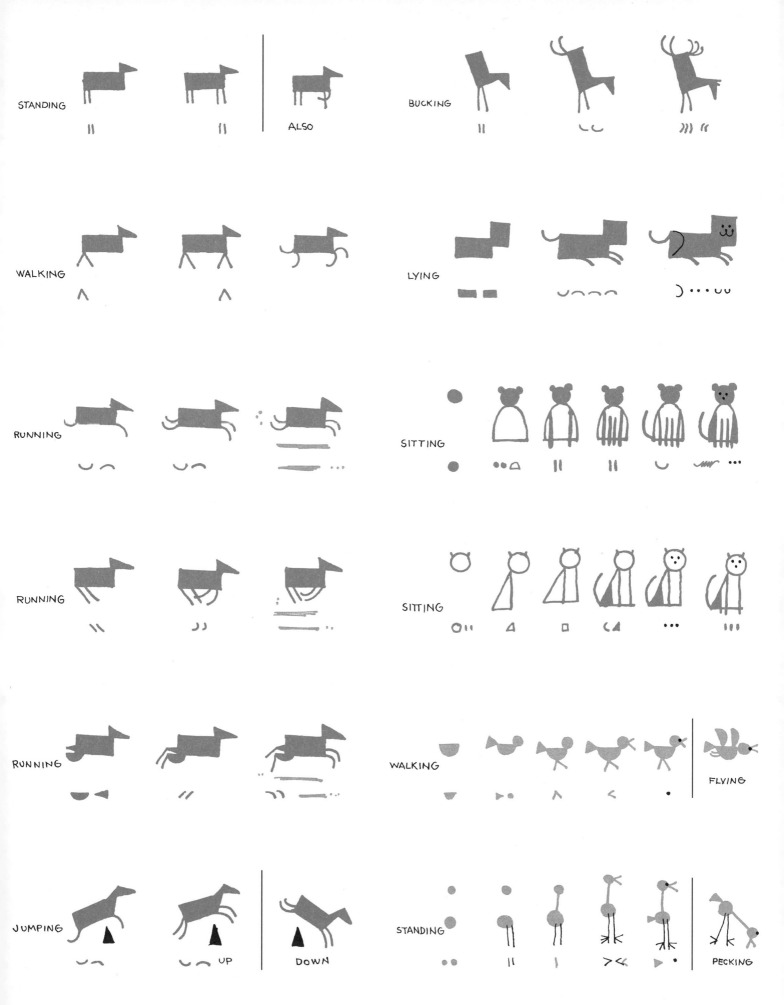

STANDING

ALSO

BUCKING

WALKING

LYING

RUNNING

SITTING

RUNNING

SITTING

RUNNING

WALKING

FLYING

JUMPING

UP

DOWN

STANDING

PECKING

YOU CAN USE FACES TO MAKE ALL KINDS OF GOOD STUFF, SUCH AS

CARDS, SIGNS, POSTERS, LETTERS, MASKS, PUPPETS, AND DOLLS.

COPYING IS ONE WAY TO LEARN HOW TO DRAW.
I HOPE YOU ENJOY TRYING TO DRAW "MY WAY,"
WILL CONTINUE TO DRAW "YOUR WAY"
AND KEEP LOOKING FOR NEW WAYS.
HAPPY DRAWING!

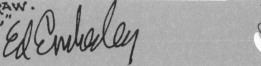

Ed Emberley

·INDEX·

* FACES STARRED CAN BE
CHANGED FROM MALE TO
FEMALE OR VICE VERSA
BY MERELY CHANGING
THE NAME. FOR INSTANCE,
"MARTIAN MARTIN" COULD
BE CHANGED TO
MARTIAN MARCIA.